STUCK ON Y J

Flairs and Glairs
Publication House

"Stuck on You"

ISBN No: " 978-93-91302-36-8"
1st Edition
Language – English and Hindi

Flairs and Glairs
Publication House
Regd. Under MSME Act.

Disclaimer

This is a work of fiction and solely represent the thoughts of the corresponding authors of the articles. Our editors have tried their best to edit the content of all the authors and check the plagiarism.
All the write-ups in this book are unique and are only published in this book.
In case any plagiarism or error is found, only the author is responsible alone, and not the publisher or the Compilers.

Cover Designing and Book Formatting
Shubham Shah and Ishani Agarwal

Acknowledgement

Compiling this anthology was an opportunity proved to be more rewarding that we could ever imagine! Foremost I extend our thanks to the Great Almighty, the author of knowledge and wisdom, for his countless love.

This book is based on experiences, thoughts and ideas of many individuals, from far and near, who took an opportunity to be a part of this book. THANKYOU. dear co-authors for building a strong foundation for the anthology. Special gratitude to our family who supported me in the entire course and friends,Ayush Shrivastava, Mehak Kesharwani, Princy Lodhi, Arya Ojha for helping me to reach many writers who wished to showcase their writing talents.

To all the relatives and friends, who in one way or other lend their helping hand for the completion of this work, we thank you! Concluding, by acknowledging, the readers, who will read this collection and inspire us to write even more. Last but most important, a ton of thanks to our publication "Flairs and Glairs", who showed immense faith in us, and to fulfil the dream of being a published author.

Preface

No man is an island.
Anthology is weaved around attachment. In our life, we bump into variety of eyes, out of those some become the labyrinth we lost in, those souls swizzle our heart. To all those people who have come across our life and left their imprints behind, who are no longer in touch with us but who dwell in our memories since the moment they left us, we are still living that time when they bid us an unasked farewell, we are still stuck in that moment. Also, the people to whom our feelings have not been expressed, this book covers the sentiments of love, the pleasure of eyes "crush", the state of attraction "attachment", and the connectivity in form of words.

Co-Authors

Shubham Shah (Founder Flairs And Glairs)
Ishani Agarwal (Co-Founder Flairs And Glairs)
Sumit Sharma{Compiler}

1. Aditi Nahar Jain
2. Nidhi Khushhal
3. Spoorthi Hc
4. Princy Lodhi
5. Adelheid Hisie Alimpuyo
6. Shaily Saroj
7. Swathi C
8. Antim Engle
9. Aliya Khan
10. Nakshatra Mala Das
11. Rakhi Gosain
12. Bhoomika Basavaraj
13. Shreshta Thakre
14. Manisha Gayathri
15. Arya Ojha
16. Aditi Jaiswal
17. Harsh Sharma
18. Tripti Pandey
19. Priyanka Dhiver
20. Raghav Chauhan
21. Ranajoy Biswas (Musafir)
22. Arshi Zaman
23. Sarabjot Purba
24. Reynu
25. Shivani Prajapati
26. Shalili B. S.
27. Ayushi Raghuwanshi

28. Shahid Patel
29. Arpita Kawde
30. Vishakha Malukani (Morika)
31. Prakhar Nema
32. Niharika N Jain
33. Afifa Sharif
34. Yachika Rathore
35. Sudipta
36. Mohana Priya.S.K
37. Aliya Siddiqua
38. Mausam Agrawal
39. Dikshita Singh
40. Ajay Gupta
41. Mohana Priya K
42. Shriyansh Jain
43. Adarsh Pandey
44. Amit Pandit
45. Poonam Chaudhary
46. Simmy
47. Divas Vishwajana
48. Hetavi Singh
49. Prachi Sharma
50. Manya Bansal

Shubham Shah

(Founder- Flairs and Glairs)

Shubham Shah, an entrepreneur at "Flairs & Glairs" a brand with dynamics in events organizing and cultural educational pan INDIA, is a 26yrs old guy who recently has entered the digital platform of imprinting emotions. He has initiated with his own open mic platform to help budding poets and aspiring writers under his brand named as "Teekhe Zasbaaat"

He is a commerce graduate from the Bhagalpur City of Bihar. He states Writing has impersonated him since childhood and he has now been writing for over a decade!
Cooking, on the other hand, is his passion! He also mentions, trying out new things just tickles him!
When asked sir, Why SPICY EMOTIONS?
He smiled and added, "agar jasbaat teekhe na ho toh wo jasbaat kahan" Spices are all that blends! So do his words!
As a chef, he presents to you his dish! Hot and freshly served! Taste it! Feel it! Enjoy it! You can also find his writing in the Book "Teekhe Zasbaaat" and 50+ Co-authored anthologies. With his passion to explore opportunities across Platforms, he is working with keen devotion and We wish him all the very best for his future ventures.
He is Featured in the International Magazine DeMode for his upcoming solo novel.
He is Approved by Ne8x for its Lit Fest, and is a Golden Star Awards 2020 Winner.
He is a India Book of Records Holder for his Anthology Satrang, and has the Grandmaster title by Asia Book of Records, for the same.
He has also been featured in Prabhat Khabar, Dainik Jagran, and a lot of other Newspapers in Bihar for his achievements.
He has been a proud co-author to
India Book Of Records (Title- Black)
World Book Of Records (Title -15 Wonders of Poetries)
India Book Of Records (Title - Aaina)
Vajra World Records Holder (Title - Gustakhi Maaf Hai)
High Range of Records Holder (Title - Gustakhi Maaf Hai)
Indian Book of Records
(Title - Road from Worst to Best)

Share your reviews on his

INSTAGRAM

@spicy_emotions
@shubham4shah

Or via email on

shubham2shah@gmail.com

To stay tuned to his work and opportunities follow his business Handles

INSTAGRAM FACEBOOK YOUTUBE

@flairsandglairs
@teekhezasbaaat

WEBSITE:

https://flairsandglairs.in/
https://flairsandglairs.com/

Ishani Agarwal

(Co-Founder- Flairs and Glairs)

Ishani Agarwal hails from the City of Joy, Kolkata.
She is the co-founder of her Community "Teekhe Zasbaaat" and Flairs and Glairs Publication.
Been a Compiler for 45+ Anthologies, she is in the process for more. Co-authored in 150+ Anthologies. She is a India Book of Records Holder, a Vajra World Records Holder, a High Range of Records Holder, an OMG Book of Records Holder, a Bravo Record holder, a Forever Star Book of World Records and an Indian Book of Records Holder.
Approved by Ne8x for its Lit Fest 2020, and Literary Icon 2020. Also a Golden Star Awards Winner 2020.
She has also been awarded with India Star Republic Award 2021, a part of She Awards by Awards Arc and Winner of Nari Samman 2021 by Literoma.

She is also selected as Best Achiever of the Year by AwardsArc and Most Challenging Compiler Award by Spectrum Awards.
She got her first solo Published,a solo Compilation consisting of first 750 contents of hers, titled "Hand That Burnt While Healing".

She has been featured by the National Magazine "Taree Zameen Par" with the title 'unstoppable'.
Also featured in the International Magazine DeMode for her upcoming solo novel, she is proud to write on social issues, and is happy with the love she is receiving.
Connect with her on Instagram: @Ishani_agarwal_quotes / @compilations_so_far

Sumit Sharma

Sumit Sharma is published writer and compiler, Contributed in many anthologies. He hails from town of Madhya Pradesh named Ganj Basoda , belongs to Bhopal division. He is Attaining qualification in pharmaceutical sciences. *Elysian_an eye shower* is his first compilation of the year 2020. He is extremely fond of learning new things. He is versatile and believe in exploring self. Apart from writing he has keen interest in acting and dancing. ***The Radius, seven essence*** are some of his compilations.

Aditi Nahar Jain

Aditi is an aspiring writer who lives vicariously through her words.
She is born and brought up in Seoni (Madhya Pradesh)
An introvert, collector of pens, who spends most of her time with coffee and books; searching the path to Alchemy of words and language of Universe.
An orator, who ironically believes in staying silent and letting her writings speak.

Embrace of Love

Sitting by the window
Watching the orange pink hues of sky
Hot piping coffee in the hand
Your thoughts in my mind

We've been meeting daily
My morning routine includes gazing you
And evenings pass by remembering the gaze
Reminiscing about what I could have done different

The way you press your teeth against each other,
Because you believe that's what makes your smile pretty
The way you caress your own wavy hairs
Because that makes you feel a little less stressed

I've been lurking
Your hand eye coordination
When you play the perfect rhythm
With those drums, nothing but best

I've seen how you get so playful
Finding rhythm in nature
Getting inspired by every little thing
Making everyone smile around you

We haven't held hands
Yet somehow, I could feel every inch of skin
feeling the warmth and electric impulses
Running in every direction, with just the thought of it

I've been drunk dialling you
And I know we've expressed our love over a million times

Yet pretending that we haven't
Because we're too afraid of our own feelings

I'm unsure of almost everything
But one thing that I've never been surer of
This is the time I stop running,
From the love, that has found home in my heart

From my feelings, from you
This is the time I'll run towards you
With a hope that you'll catch me
Embrace me with your warm love

Nidhi Khushhal

Nidhi Khushhal is a neet 2021 aspirant. She is fond of writing. Basically, she's interested in writing articles, shayries & poems including even Urdu words is her major interest. But as per the need she anyhow manages to write whatever required for the theme. She is currently residing in Indore "the food city" and "the cleanest city" of Madhya Pradesh.. Soon She'll be doing MBBS just a few steps away from her dream. She also has keen interest in music (listening as well as singing) and musical instruments, sometimes cooking. She is Inspired by her favorite writer Gulzar Sahab, Waseem Barelvi, Ghalib, Amish Tripathi and more.

लगाव

एक ऐसा एहसास जिस पर लाख कोशिशों के बावजूद हम विजय नहीं पा सकते॥ सबसे ज्यादा इसका एहसास तब होता है, जब पराए शहर की सड़कों पर आदमी अकेला चल रहा होता है। उन सन्नाटों में वो खुद को ऐसे महसूस करता है मानो शाम ढले रेत के ढेर में कोई जुगनू अपने होने की इत्तिला कर रहा हो॥ जब रात में सोने से पहले सारी बत्तियां बुझाने के बाद कोई खिड़की खुली रह जाए और उससे आ रही मध्धम सी रोशनी उसे अपनेपन का बोध करा रही हो, वह आकर उसके कानों में धीरे से कहती है कि, यहां उसका कोई नहीं सिवाय उसके जो अंधियारों से घिरी रात में कुछ वक्त के लिए उसका सहारा बन जाती है फिर उसे याद आते हैं अपने जिनसे उसे इतना लगाव होता है कि एक फोन की घंटी सुनने बस को वो सारा दिन इंतजार करता है क्योंकि उसे उन सब से लगाव होता है। यह लगाव ही तो है जो हम सबको जोड़े रखता है, एक अटूट बंधन में बांधे रखता है। कुछ ऐसा ही लगाव मुझे भी है.. मेरे घर से, मेरे शहर से, मेरे अपनों से...

ये सर्द रातें, कड़कती बिजलियां, बेवफा बारिशें, बेरंग आसमां काश अपने शहर में हम होते तो घर चले जाते॥

रंगीन सवेरे और शब भर रही गलियों में मेरी छोटे से घर में जीवन संवर गया था॥

अनजान सड़कें, सफर दूर का, ये आवारगी, ये तन्हाई हम अपने शहर में होते तो घर चले जाते॥

वो बचपन की यादें, खिलोनो का ढेर, दोस्तों की महफ़िल आंसुओं को वहाँ किनारा मिल जाता था॥

जिम्मेदारियों का बोझ, लोगों से तकरार, एहसान ज़माने के, हम अपने बंदों में होते तो घर चले जाते॥

बूढ़े मां बाप की डांट, समझाईशें हजार, वहां रोते तो रोने पर सहारा मिल जाता था||

ये दूसरों की पहचान, शोर ज़माने का, ये गैर पन और तपिश दर्द की, कि हम अपनों में होते तो घर चले जाते||

Spoorthi Hc

Spoorthi H C is a writer from Chikkamagaluru, Karnataka with over 30 anthologies published as a co-author. She began writing while still a student and aspires to be a full-time writer someday. She is a classical singer and dancer. By profession, she is an engineer but by passion, she is an expressive writer. She also writes in Kannada and has her work published in various newspapers and magazines from time to time. She also publishes her Kannada poetry on Instagram @kavithegala_saalu and her English poetries on @narrowsea_stories. An optimistic, unique individual with an infectious smile and a generous heart. Spoorthi assumes that words provide the best comfort at all times. Recently she awarded the "Nammura Nakshatra" state-level award for her contribution to the literature field.

Oh, My Dear Crush!

A Morning of misty breeze,
Jogging cloud in the winter,
My heart slowly began to wheeze,
Peeing to your elegance smile,
I decided to walk with you a mile,
Defying all my nightmare for a while,
With a gleam of devotion in my mind,
And divine love in my dreamy land.

Oh, My Dear Crush!
You're a handsome man,
Generous gentleman,
An Authentic identity,
And a seductive personality,
I found that one heart in the zillion,
Yet you are in my impression,
Only for you, my love survives,
Nourishing you in my happiness,
Catching a glimpse of you in my victories.

Oh, My Dear Crush!
I knew our first formal meet,
While I was a bit impatient,
Later I found a companion in you,
Get moulded vast faith from you,
I saw your care towards the creatures,
I saw your responsibilities towards the work,
I saw your affection toward your family,
You're an extraordinary human being,
With a hell of humour living,

Oh, My dear Crush!

When you glowed with me,
Saw a cherishing bird inside me,
You're a valuable soul,
You're a venerable individual,
You guided me when I'm intense,
You assisted me when I'm in fortune,
My love is Eternal for you,
My compassion is perpetual to you,
My entity is only for you.

Princy Lodhi

Princy Lodhi, who hails from Sagar (Madhya Pradesh), is currently pursuing her undergraduate course in pharmacy. Apart from writing, she loves to do craftworks. She pens down her thoughts on paper, through poems. Her recent published work includes "The Radius" where she had been a compiler as well as co-author. She believes that writing helps one in easing out their feelings and understanding oneself better.

Mine

Dear Love,
I might not be that good with looks, but i know our happiness will be beautiful together. I might not be an ideal figure lady but the figures of our life together will be so. I might not be an early morning person but our mornings will have sunshine together. I might not be punctual but you'll never regret the time spent together. I might not get sarcasm for once, but it would be fun for us to be together. I might not be good at memorising, but whenever you'll turn the life's book, best memories would be ours. I might be a short height person but i know our relationship will last the longest. I might be going places but my heart will stay stuck on you. I know I'm a procrastinator but these things would be true if you'll say a yes right now?
I don't belong to anyone as such, but will you be mine?

Permanent

Through all thoughts in dark,
you are my ray of hope.
When i fall off the expectation's cliff,
you are my motivating rope.
Amidst the blaming crowd,
you are my person to trust.
To decorate my colourless life,
you are the golden dust.
Vanishing the foul essence of hatred,
you are my lovable scent.
In this temporary world,
you are my permanent.

Adelheid Hisie Alimpuyo

She is a 14 years old girl from the Philippines.

"For You"

Those eyes that were sparkling a lot
Those smiles that fluttering my heart
To the one who always stands out in the crowd
To a man who has a soft and pure heart.

For you who will never know my name
For you who didn't know my existence
I will take all your agonies and pain
I will stay by your side until the end.

The tears are falling again
As I pray for you
I hope it flies to you
My words that will always be unheard.

For you who cannot see me
For you who cannot hear me
I will wait for you until the sun dies
I will wish for you until the end of time.

For you who makes the sun brighter
For you who gave me inspiration
For you who I will support eternally
For you who I will love unconditionally.

Shaily Saroj

She is Shaily Saroj from Sangam nagri Prayagraj..She is 19 year's old. She is a college student of Allahabad University. She is a new writer. Through poetries she wants to express her inner feelings. Her hobbies are poetry writing, singing and reading novels...Her top priority is Family.

कुछ बाते

कुछ बाते देखो जाना हम कहां आ गए,
टूटते- टूटते देखो हम कैसे बिखर गए,
जाते जाते ये कैसा जख्म अदा कर गए,
दिल पर ये कैसा सितम कर गए,
तेरे जाने से ये दुनिया बेगानी लगती है,
आंखे भी अपने दर्द की कहानी लिखती है,
जाना कोई ऐसी रात नहीं गई,
जब तेरी यादों ने मेरे पलकों को भिगाया ना हो,
अब तो नींद और सपनों से भी डर सा लगने लगा है,
कोई और अब तेरे करीब आएगा,
ये सोचकर हर पल सहम जाया करती हूं,
जो जख्म तूने दिल को अदा किया है वो अब कभी भरेगा नहीं,
तुझे तो ये महज एक कहानी लगती,
तेरी गलियों से हमारा गुजरना अब हमें हमारी रुसवाई लगती है,
हो जाओ कभी अगर तुम मेरी यादों से आजाद,
तो मेरे इश्क़ को एक पहचान देना,
हो जाएं अगर कभी किसी से मोहब्बत,
तो उसको मेरी नाम की पहचान ना देना।।

ये इश्क

ये इश्क तू यू मुझे ना सताया कर,
कभी तो इस दिल को भी समझाया कर,
कहता है नहीं रहना उसके बिना,
अब तू ही बता किस तरह इसकी जिद्द छुड़वाया जाए,
क्या कहा उसको वापस ले आऊ अपनी जिंदगी में,
तभी दिल धड़केगा पहले की तरह,
ये क्या कह दिया इश्क़ तूने,
क्या तू वाकिफ नहीं किस तरह था छोड़ा उसने,
बिना वजह दिए बस कह दिया कोई रिश्ता नहीं निभाना तेरे साथ,
रोती थी दिन-रात तिल तिल कर मरती थी हर पल,
पर वो कहां सुनने वाला था,
हां बेशक वाकिफ था वो मेरी इस हालत से,
फिर भी न पूछा कभी हाल मेरा,
ना पूछ ये इश्क किस तरह खुद को संभाला था,
आंखों में आंसू लेकर कैसे होठों से मुस्कुराया था,
निकल जाता था पूरा दिन खुद को संभालते संभालते,
और रात मे फिर उसकी यादों में टूट के बिखर जाया करते थे,
मत रो ये दिल कोशिश करती हूं उसको वापस लाने की,
क्या कहा नहीं चाहिए अब वो,
क्यों क्या हुआ आधी दर्द - ए - दास्तां में ही आंख भर आई,
अभी तो पूरी दर्द - ए - दास्तां सुनानी बाकी है ।।।।

Swathi C

She is an engineering student and a young writer who write poems and quotes to heal the wounded hearts. Love for rhythm of words, feel of words and rhyme words are much beyond the infinity for her.

26 Alphabets Of Love

Attachment is love
Blithe is love
Care is love
Devotion is love
Emotion is love
Forbearance is love
Generous is love
Hankering is love
Inexpressible is love
Joyful is love
Kind is love
Look after is love
Mushy is love
Never been better is love
Over protective is love
Patience is love
Quiet is love
Romantic is love
Soulful is love
Together is love
Union is love
Vent is love
Warmth is love
Xany is love
Yearn is love
Zest is love

My Promise

The trees may stop giving air,
But I will never stop showering you my care.
The cloud may stop giving rain,
But I will never stop shielding you from pain.
The sea may stop wavering one day,
But I will always keep your problems at bay.
The stars may stop to twinkle,
But I will never stop you to mingle.
The sun may stop shining like a gold,
But I will be with you till I get old
The moon may stop to shimmer,
But I will be your lover forever.

Antim Engle

Antim Engle is a schooling girl studying in 11th standard. Her current residence is sanawad. "Articulating is like seeing my on reflection in pages."

"Dear Crush"

बिन सफर बिन मंजिल सा ये रास्ता,
जंगल का ठहरा सा वो दरिया,
उन चकाचौंध आंखों का दिखना ,
पल में हि पलकें भिग जाना ,
तुम्हे पुरा लिखुं ये सोचना,
पर कुछ शब्दो में हि बवाल हो जाना,
धूप तो लोट जाती है मायुस होकर,
तू छत पर आया कर,
दिल ना सही हाथ हि मिलायाकर,
तुम्हे चाहा इतना कि किसी और को चाहने कि चाहत ना रही,
यु तो मुहब्बत की हकीकत से वाकिफ हुं,
पर तुम्हें देखा तो सोचा,
खुद को बर्बाद ही कर लु।

Aliya Khan

Aliya Khan, writes poetry, which, considering where you are reading this, makes perfect sense. She is best known for her poetry, hindi shayari and small write ups on life. She is a teacher by profession and currently living abroad in the UAE. She hails from the city of Mumbai where she completed her Bachelors in Commerce before she went abroad to pursue her Masters qualifications and settled there. To read more of her write ups you can visit her blog on Instagram @poetry_byak.

What You Are To Me!

You are friendly, kind and caring,
Sensitive, loyal and understanding
Humorous, fun, secure and true
Always there... Yes thats you.

Special, accepting, exciting and wise,
Truthful and helpful with honest eyes,
Confiding, forgiving, cheerful and bright,
Yes thats you... Not one bit of spite.

You're one of a kind, different from others,
Generous, charming, but not one that smothers.
Optimistic, thoughtful, happy and game
But not just another... In the long chain.

Appreciative, warm and more precious than gold,
Our love wont tarnish or ever grow old.
You'll always be there, I know that is true,
I'll always be here... Always for you.

Beauty, joy and grace with which you have filled my life,
And made the world I live in a better and happier place.
Without you. I know I shall die.

You Are Really Special!

You are my smile,
As you were the first who made me do so.
You are my eyes,
As you have given me tears of joy.
You are my happiness,
As from you I learned to laugh.
You are my friend,
As everytime you are there to comfort me.
You are my heart,
As it beats only for you.
You are my breath,
As you make me realize how important I am to you.
You are my memories,
Which are sweet and colorful.
You are my thoughts
As I only think of you.
You are my words,
As you are always on my tounge.
You are my need,
As I am desperate about you.
You are my moon,
As you light up my sky.
You are my life
As I love it because of you in it.
You are my love,
As you have taught me the meaning of it.
You are in me,
As everywhere I sense you.
You are someone really special to me!

Nakshatra Mala Dash

She is Nakshatra Mala Dash a girl who lives in Bhubaneswar Odisha. She is a girl whose eyes are full of dreams and hopes. She has been a co-author in few anthologies. Also, her own e-book (At Last you're mine) has been published. She believes in becoming a better person every day. She loves to write. To know more about her you can follow her on instagram i.e, @weaving_word.

The Attachment

My attachment with you was bit different than others.
The day you smiled, made my mood joyous.
The day you remained sad, made me pissed off.
The day you remained absent; your pictures made me felt your presence.
The day when everyone else noticed your anger, I noticed your tears.
The day when everyone else noticed your smile, I noticed your unspoken pain behind it.
The day when everyone else stood against you, I remained beside you.
The day when everyone else kept on scolding you, I kept on holding you.
The day when everyone else waved you a good bye, I simply sighed.
When everyone else cried on your farewell day, my heart screamed that day.
Perhaps my attachment with you was bit different than others.

Rakhi Gosain

We would like to introduce Rakhi Gosain as a new author in the town. Mirror Talk (Each Question Has A Different Voice) is her first published poem (in fiction) in an Anthology named "Unvoiced Words" and she is working with us as a Co-author in our new project "Stuck on You" and other two anthologies. She believes that writing is the best way to kick the stress out from your life even when a pandemic tries to turn everything shut down and she says "writing gives you a stage where you can set your thoughts free to dance and speak candidly."We wish her Good Luck for her upcoming undertakings.

Instagram: @myflyingnotes
Email: gosain.rakhi92@gmail.com

I Am After You

I find beauty in abundance,
glory and luster is everywhere,
I don't lack with people who adore me,
But I never get it...why do I always choose going after you.
Mailbox is full of well wishes,
They write letters to me like crazy,
Rings and bended knees are no rare,
But I never get it...why do I always choose going after you.
Never experienced scarcity of mates,
Who don't want reasons to celebrate,
Colliding cocktails with friends I like too,
But I never get it...why do I always choose going after you.
Casual greetings with beating hearts,
Messages loaded with roses and flirt,
They try to persuade and make me respond,
But I never get it...why do I always choose going after you.

The Proposal

If love had a body, it would have been you,
Like a compulsory subject I will definitely pursue,
It doesn't matter how many times I fail,
One thing is for sure that this is what I'm gonna do.

Can you even think, how do you make me feel?
Being near you kicks my soreness to heal,
When you look into my eyes, I want to put up a question,
Can stealing a heart be this big deal???

I know you are aware, our quietness speaks a lot,
We both are tied up with an invisible knot,
I've been trying for so long, hope this time I'm doing it right,
I hold my ears and apologize if it takes more than one shot.

I promise always and forever, I'll be there for you,
However, you are not prepare but can I expect this too,
My feet seem jammed, could you please help?
it's hard to move on alone, sweetheart I'm stuck on you.

Bhoomika Basavaraj

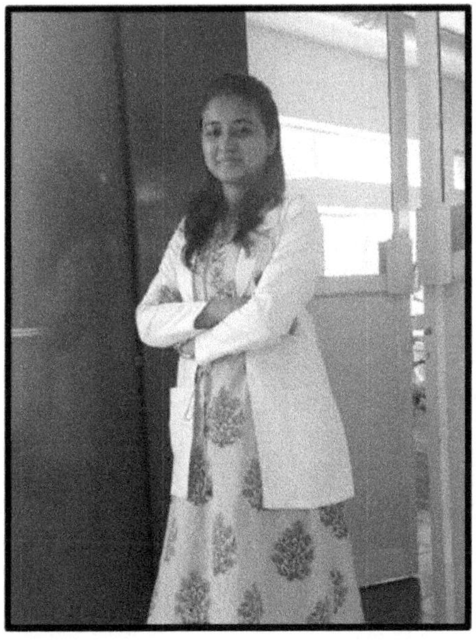

A girl from chikmagalur , saw the real world in mangalore and who became a doctor as desired . And who loves to write .

Crush

Your voice is beautiful,
And can hear it all day long.

Your long talks,
make me realize that cuteness is real.

Your smile is contagious,
And can make me forget everything else.

Your one look,
Can make my day.

Your touch,
Can make me completely happy.

Shreshtha Thakre

She is shreshtha thakre from raigarh chhattisgarh. She is graduated from pt. Ravishankar university, Raipur. Now she is in indore madhya pradesh. She writers to express and motivate. She is nothing more than a girl who choose herself above anything.

Quotes

Loving him was her choice but choosing him to love her is not.

वह जिस्म की प्यास को रोगी मोहब्बत समझती रही,
उसने जिस्म की प्यास बुझा उसके रूहू को तार-तार कर दिया

Manisha Gayathri

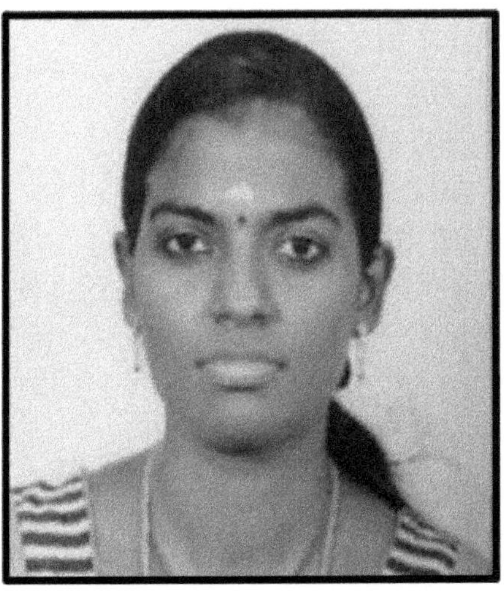

Manisha Gayathri,A creative and inspirational writer who pens down her feelings and thoughts for the sake of the society. She is a poetry lover and believes in the magical power of words.

एक प्यार ऐसा भी ....

तुमसे हमारी चाहत है कितनी
यह नही है जानते हम .....
चाहत तुम्हारी भी कम नही ,
यह तो है जानते हम .....
दिल में तुम्हारी , अपनी जगह
यह भी है जानते हम ....
ख्याल भी न है हमारा , ये जताना
यह भी है जानते हम .....
हमसे दूरी के ख्याल से भी, आँखें
नम कर जाते हो तुम ....
हर दर्द को जिद्द के मुखौटे से
छूपा जाते हो तुम .....
प्यार को चुप्पी से अपने
छुपा जाते हो तुम .....
अपनी हरखतों से अंजाने हमें
समझते हो तुम .....
सनम दिखावे से नही , वफा से
प्रभावित होते है हम ....
इक प्यार ऐसा भी, जिसका
एहसास जानते है सिर्फ हम-तुम

Arya Ojha

Arya Ojha is a poetess. She loves to write and recite poetry. Anchoring, Crafting is other combination of her hobbies. She had participated in 10 Anthologies as a
Co-author and has compiled books named “Elysian- my eye shower”, "The Memory Land", "Sunshine".

हमारा साथ

वो लम्हे तुम्हारे साथ ,
वो प्यार भरे जज्बात,
वो हाथो में हाथ ,
वो इश्क़ का नया सा पैग़ाम,
वो तुम्हारा मेरे पास आना,
वो तुम्हारा मेरा नाम पुकारना,
वो जब तुमने दिल को छुआ,
वो जब तुमने अपना बनाया,
वो तुमसे यू प्यार हो जाना,
वो आंखो ही आंखो में बात हो जाना,
वो तुम्हारी आहटें,
वो तुम्हारे मुस्कुराहटें,
वो तुम्हारा मुझमें समाना,
वो तुम्हारा मेरे अस्तितव को महसूस करना,
वो हमारा साथ बन जाना,
वो हमारा दास्तां आज जाना।

Aditi Jaiswal

Aditi loves to write on love, friendship, women empowerment, heartbreak, power , motherhood . She is the published author of many books in which she has pen down her heart. She lives in Varanasi and you can contact her on Instagram as __ajcreations__

पहली बूंद

तू मौसम की पहली बारिश सा
मैं बारिश की उस बूंद सी
तेरे आने से मेरा आना
और
तेरे जाते ही मेरा खत्म हो जाना
ना जाने कैसी फितरत है मेरी
तुझसे शुरू और तुझ में ही खत्म हो जाना

Harsh Sharma

Somewhere far far from Gusty waves, in the love rocked caves, someone is dreaming that humanity is still not a myth. Harsh Sharma, people call him. Happily swinging in his poetic world, he also admires to be a content creator on Instagram. The chap belonging from Haryana has huge dream to be best selling novelist. To know more about him:

Instagram: author_harsharma
Mail: sharmaharsh24122000@gmail.com

Oh, Unfortunate Love!

We're facing each other,
Right into the teary eyes.

I'm with my spouse,
You're with yours.

Feeling like hugging you,
Expecting the same from you.

Hardly matters we are in pain,
We tried to be one, but all in vain.

We stalked each other,
Our families didn't.

We loved each other,
our castes didn't.

हजामत-ए-मोहब्बत

कुछ यूं बेहया मशहूर मोहब्बत हमारी हो गई,
जब पलकें झुकाई उन्होंने और इबादत हमारी हो गई।

नज़रें मिलाने से ज्यादा हमने कहां कुछ मांगा था,
वो खामखां हंस दिए और बदनाम शराफत हमारी हो गई।

चेहरे से निगाहें हटती, तब तो जिस्म का मुआयना करते,
उनकी आंखों की चमक से जिंदगी क़यामत हमारी हो गई।

और फिर हिज्र की क्या बात करे, दिल टूटा नहीं, चूरा चूरा हो गया,
वो कहां गए, कब गए, कोई खबर नहीं....

खबर तो बस नाई-ए-दिल की चीख हमें दे रही थी कि
इश्क लड़ाने के खेल में,
गलत हजामत हमारी हो गई।

Tripti Pandey

Tripti Pandey, born and brought up in Bhadohi district of Uttar Pradesh. Birthday is on 30th August (19teen) to the father Virendra Kumar Pandey and mother Madhu Pandey. Right now she's neet aspirant with intermediate Bachelorette degree 2020 (science stream) from Small Wonders sr. sec. School Jabalpur. She started writing when she was in class seventh since then she's penning down her emotions and deep thought and eventually her goal is to bring a change by her writings.

।। अधूरी सी कहानी मेरी ।।

अधूरी सी जिंदगानी मेरी,
तू ही अधूरी सी कहानी मेरी।
टूट गई हूं तुझ बिन,
अधूरी सी ये राहें मेरी।
टूट कर चाहा तुझे,
तू अधूरे मंजर की अधूरी कहानी मेरी।
तुझ बिन जीना सीखा ही नहीं,
मेरे अंत की अधूरी कहानी तूही।
तड़पते धड़कन की तू अधूरी ख्वाहिश मेरी,
तलब तूही उपाय तूही।
आजा लौट कर तुझ बिन अधूरी सी राहत मेरी,
पूरे मर्ज की दवाई तूही।
राह भी बंजर सी,
अधूरी मंजर की कहानी तूही।
भटक रही हूं इंतजार में तेरे,
मेरे अधूरे मौत की पूरी कहानी तूही।

रिश्ते की डोर

अरे! अरे! संभालकर रिश्ते की डोर है, थोड़ी नाजुक है।
प्यार और भरोसे जैसी महंगी कपास से बनी डोर है।
आगे समय की नुकीली धार है और बदलते भावनाओं की मार है।
ना झोंको ज्वलनशील करवाहटो में, करवाहटे सुलगती आग हैं।
जल जाएगी रिश्ते की डोर आगे करवाहटो की ताप है।
सजगता जैसी गहराइयों को समझना रिश्ते की डोर संभाल कर पकड़ना,
टूट जाते हैं अक्सर नासमझी के कारण,
ऐसी नासमझी तुम ना करना।

Priyanka Dhiver

Priyanka dhiver resides in Mumbai .she is a B. A graduate. As we know ,there are many things that we feel like, sorrow, anger, love, pain.there are many people who cannot get out of them ,so priyanka writes for the people. besides she writes what she feels.

दिल का कनेक्शन

धड़कता है यह दिल, आने की आहट से आपके
बहती है सांसे आपकी, तिष्णगी के एहसास के आपके।
यह दिल का कनेक्शन कुछ यूं आपसे है हमारा, जो बयाना हो पाती कुछ लफ्जों से
सुबह कि वह बेदर्द शभा कुछ इस तरह रूम में समा जाती है
जैसे गुल खिल जाते हैं गुलशन में दरमियां हमारे कुछ अनोखा सा रिश्ता है।
वह फितरत इश्क की तुम हो, उल्फत हूं मैं तुम्हारी।
जुड़ी है जिंदगी आपकी और हमारी प्यार की डोर से,
इस डोर का कनेक्शन जुड़ा है एक रूह की डोर से।

Raghav Chauhan

Raghav Chauhan is a Published author. He was born on 06th July 1997 at Moradabad, UP. His original name is Ramakant Singh. His writing journey has started from Haridwar and he has suffered many challenges in his life because he belongs to a middle-class family. He has written 2 solo, compiled 3 books and co-authored in 40 anthologies.
He's 8times record holder and also featured in international newspaper MT Kenya times. You can contact him on IG - @unprofessional_writer_raghav
Twitter - Raghav Chauhan
Facebook - Raghav Chauhan YQ App - Raghav Chauhan

Midnight Memory

Your name upon my lips,
Your vision on my mind
Asking a relentless question
With no answer there to find.

Ah, but my heart does pulse
And keep a stately time
With the syllables of your name
Mouthed by a talkative mime

And as I stroll through my thoughts
One thing I do keep near
It's the gentle caress of your words
As you say, I love you dear. "

I Want Nothing More Than You...

I want to pour,
My love for you,
All over your body,
And into your soul.

I want to give,
You all I can,
My heart is for you,
My life in your hands.

I want everyone,
To see that we're one,
Nothing can come between us,
We've become one soul.

Ranajoy Biswas (Musafir)

काव्य की माया भोग से परे, है त्याग को समर्पित|
त्यागी स्वयं हृदय अपना... शब्दरूप मे करता है अर्पित||
-मुसाफिर

काव्य की इसी माया की खोज मे नबयुवक शायर 'रणजय बिश्वास' ऊर्फ 'मुसाफिर' ने अपने बिद्यार्थी जीवन मे ही हिंदी एबं उर्दू साहित्य की कलाई थामी। शायरी, कविताएं, एबं छोटी रचनाओं के साथ साहित्य की यथा सम्भब सेवा की। अपने गृहनगर मे स्थित कोलकाता बिश्वविद्यालय के स्नातक 'मुसाफिर' अपनी छोटी रचनाओं के संकलन इंस्टाग्राम पे @musafir_ki_yaadein पर प्रकाशित भी करते है।

नादान...

दिल की जगह, जो है नज़रे चुरा रही...
इस क़दर भी, वह अनजान तो न थी...
नाराज़गी को मेरी, नफरत समझ बैठे,
इस कदर भी, वह नादान तो न थी।

चिराग ए मोहब्बत मेहफ़ूज़ थी बहोत...
हवाओ से झगड़कर, उसे संभाला करता था।
निगाहो से इज़हार, कभी कर चूका था शायद,
बस लब्ज़ो मे कहने से डरता था।

खामोशियाँ भी कुछ कर न पायी बयाँ?
इस कदर भी चाहत... बेजुबान तो न थी...
नाराज़गी को, मेरी, नफरत समझ बैठे,
इस कदर भी, वह नादान तो न थी।

शिकवा नहीं अब कोई, उनसे...
जो तन्हा यूं, मुझे कर गई।
यादें मेहफ़ूज़ उस ख्वाब की अब भी है,
जो खुद टूट कर बिखर गई।

बिखरे, उन ख़्वाबों पर तक़दीर मेरी,
इस कदर भी, मेहरबान तो न थी।
नाराज़गी को, मेरी, नफरत समझ बैठे,
इस कदर भी, वह नादान तो न थी।

सितम से अब समझौता सा है...
उनकी यादें भी अब, नहीं रुलाती है।
मुस्कुराहट वह, तस्वीर बनी निगाहो पे जो...
आज भी यूं ही पास बुलाती है।

अनकहे उन लफ्ज़ो को सुन ले...
ज़िन्दगी, मोहब्बत की इतनी कदरदान तो न थी।
नाराज़गी को, मेरी, नफरत समझ बैठे,
इस कदर भी, वह नादान तो न थी।

Arshi Zaman

This is Arshi Zaman. She's currently pursuing Masters in English Literature and is very fond of writing as her words are the portrayal of the vehemence her heart possesses.

My First Peculiar Heartbeat!

That vehemence was never felt before,
The one I felt for you tonight.
I had obliterated to smile for days, months and years,
But today again, after ages, I beheld myself smile!

My heart skipped a beat when, you passed by my side.
I endeavoured to conceal the sparkle in my eyes.
I essayed to be rigorous but even failed to do so.

My eyes then peered into your soul,
And conveyed a note of love.
I had loved eagles long back,
But now I loved the white doves.

The glaze of my love since then,
Never visited the dark, old me.
I fell in love with the chaos of life,
Since then, it was you, all around that I could see.

Sarabjot Purba

सरबजोत पुरबा कोटकपूरा, पंजाब में रहते है। जब वो बारवीं कक्षा में थे तब उन्होंने पहली बार एक कविता लिखी। इसके बाद ई.टी.टी. की पढ़ाई करते समय उन्होंने कविताओं के साथ-साथ निबंध और कहानी भी लिखनी शुरू की। उन्होंने ने बहुत कुछ लिखा है जिनमें 'कुछ विचार' 'ई.टी.टी. कालेज का सफर' शामिल है। उन्होंने कई कहानियां लिखी है। उन्होंने हर विषय पर कुछ न कुछ लिखा है। अक्सर वो समाज के मुद्दों पर लिखते है। वे ज्यादातर पंजाबी भाषा का प्रयोग करते है।

मोहब्बत

जिस से मोहब्बत की गई हो,
उसका तो नाम भी दुआ के समान है।
जिस से मोहब्बत की गई हो,
उसकी नफरत भी प्यार के समान है।
जिस से मोहब्बत की गई हो,
उसकी खामोशी भी बातों के समान है।
जिस से मोहब्बत की गई हो,
उसकी आवाज़ भी मधुर के समान है।
जिस से मोहब्बत की गई हो,
उसका चेहरा भी भगवान के समान है।
जिस से मोहब्बत की गई हो,
उसका हमेशा के लिए रूठ जाना,
सांस खो जाने के समान है।
जिस से मोहब्बत की गई हो,
उसका हमेशा के लिए दूर जाना,
मौत आने के समान है।

Reynu

Reynu (Shradha Shintre) is someone who writes In such a way that it connects right to the heart. She has been often accused of making people cry :). Yes she brings forth hidden emotions with her writing. She dabbles in different genres like short stories, articles but primary being Poetry. She is a graduate with her Specialisation being Psychology - this goes a long way in her understanding the psyche of Human nature, observing things around her and bringing it forth in her writing. Reading being her weakness and also her strength- she loves Romance Suspense and Self Help Books

She Loves travelling and naturally runs a Travel Agency making people go where their Heart is!!!!

She has a YouTube channel and Instagram account by the name Poetry_Worth_Your _Time which helps her reach out to a vast audience!!! follow her @poetry_worth_your_time

I Know

Life is Like the colours of the rainbow
Sometimes we r high and sometimes low
But through it all u will be there 'I KNOW'
I maybe stubborn, angry or vain
And on a bad day I maybe a real pain
Through all my idiosyncrasies you will keep me sane 'I KNOW'
When everything has been topsy turvy through the day
With explanations none and nothing to say
In spite of your problems you will keep my sorrow at bay 'I KNOW'
When times have been unduly hard and tough
And the roads have been bumpy and rough
Together these roads with ease we will traverse 'I KNOW'

In moments of happiness tears I cannot hide
Through every achievement you have been by my side
In these special moments your eyes reflect a silent pride 'I KNOW'
With half the journey complete and the other half unknown
The best colors of life have yet to be shown
You will show me the colors in their best tones 'I KNOW'
When my hair will turn gray and my gait will be slow
But with serenity, wisdom and love my face will glow
Coz with u by my side old I will grow 'I KNOW'
This confidence of 'I KNOW''
Is in essence True Love 'I KNOW'

Shivani Prajapati

Shivani Prajapati, she loves writing her mind, her heart and that's she. It's not only her heart who wants to tell all these emotions but the whole world's heart.

Attachment

I miss her,
I cannot be myself, without her.
I miss her, I miss her.......
She's not beautiful as a celebrity,
but she attracts me like a gravity.
and it makes my heart flutter,
that's why I am in love with her.
I am missing her.... I am missing her....
She's not liked a sun who shine,
but she's the one who's mine.
Her every moment feels like a dove,
I will shine for her like moon above,
so, I will fit her like glove,
that's why I am in love.
I miss her, I miss her......
It was my only second meet with her,
but it looks like from ages I am with her.
I miss her,
I cannot be myself without her.
I miss her......I miss her.........

Shalini.B.S

Shalini.B.S is a literature student.Her writing style are about the real feeling,simple and understanding and joyful.She is writing in the pen name of TARA'.most of her works are based on real life she loves to listen music and interested in drawing and painting.

Try Not To Confuse Attachment With Love

Attachment is about fear and dependency,
And has more to do with love of self than
Love of another love without attachment is
The purest love because it isn't about what
Others can give you because you're empty.
It is about what you can give others
Because you're already full.

Ayushi Raghuwanshi

She is currently a student, she sees writing poem es unsaid words of her heart apart from that, she loves to writing and painting, reading books, and wanderlust.

बारिश

मौसम की पहली बारिश आकर अपना कर्ज निभा जाती है , बेरंग फिजा को रंगीन बना जाती है , ना जाने क्यों ये बारिश मुझ पे इतनी मेहरबानियां कर जाती है ....

आंसूओं का सैलाब लेकर आती है तो कभी कभी खुशियों की बाहर लाती है , ना जाने क्यों ये बारिश मुझ पे इतनी मेहरबानियां कर जाती है.......

पल भर का दिलासा झोली में डाल जाती है , तो कभी आंखो को नम कर जाती है , ना जाने क्यों ये बारिश मुझ पे इतनी मेहरबानियां कर जाती है ......

गुज़ारिश कर रही थी चंद फोहारो की वो सैलाब लेकर आती है नहीं समझती वो जज्बातों को सब कुछ वहा लेे जाती है ना जाने क्यों ये बारिश मुझ पे इतनी मेहरबानियां कर जाती है ....

सालो पड़ी किताबो के पन्ने पर भी सीलन पड़ जाती है ये अपने साथ बहुत कुछ वहा लेे जाती है ना जाने क्यों ये बारिश मुझ पे इतनी मेहरबानियां कर जाती है........

Shahid Patel

I am 2nd year medical student doing my MD from Cebu Philippines belong to middle class family lives in Panth Mundla Dewas Madhya Pradesh.

मोहब्बत

अनुराग कहूँ या प्रणय कहूँ
मै कह दु चाह या राँचना कहूँ
सम्मोह, वात्सल्य या प्रनय कहूँ
सुभगता, चाह या लय कहूँ
मै प्रीति या तुम्हे प्रीतिकर कहूँ
कहने को तो इश्क़, मोहब्बत या
प्यार कह लू
पर तुम बहुत ख़ास हो मेरे लिए
समझ नही आ रहा मै क्या कहूँ??
प्यार, मोहब्बत या इश्क़ कहूँ
या तुझे सब कुछ कहूँ??

Arpita Kawde

Arpita Kawde, she is a girl with full of Dream's
she writes what she actually experiences in her life.

My Love

My Love today I want to tell you that,
we are not in relationship,
This feeling is something else that
What I feel with you.
Whenever I am with you,
You can't imagine how secure and comfortable I feel with you.
My love you are so different from others in my life.
Many people knows me but you are the one who feels me.
No one can understand me
In the way you understand.
My soulmate your heart is so pure and beautiful
and I am so lucky that God gifted that heart to me.
I just want you,
Today, tomorrow and forever.
My sweetheart I can imagine my whole life with you,
Without you it's totally dead.
I hope you will be my first and last one.
I can't think anyone else.
I am not able to give this beautiful heart,
that I have given to you,
You are so special gift that God gives to me.
I love you because you saw me in the way no one else can ever
do.
I am silliest and happiest whenever I am with you.
I love you.

Vishakha Malukani (Morika)

Vishakha Malukani belongs to cleanest city Indore. She loves to pen down her feelings in her secret diary. She is currently pursuing MA Psychology. She have worked with NGO she is so much fascinated towards social work & working for unprivileged part of society. She is a published author her second book will be published soon.

सुनो क्या करोगी

सुनो क्या करोगी इन branded कपड़ो का जबकि उसे प्यार तुम्हारे जिस्म से नहीं दिल की खूबसूरती से हैं,
सुनो क्या करोगी ये महंगी lipsticks का जबकि प्यार तो उसे तुम्हारी मीठी दिल छू लेने वाली आवाज़ से हैं,
सुनो क्या करोगी ये महंगे kajal liner का जबकि प्यार तो उसे तुम्हारी आंखों में दिखती मासूमियत से हैं,
सुनो क्या करोगी ये महंगे iphone लेकर जबकि तुमसे बात करने के लिए उसे फोन की ज़रूरत ही नहीं हैं दिल से ही दिल की बाते हो जाती हैं ,
सुनो क्या करोगी उसके लिए 5star में birthday surprise रख कर जबकि उसे तो तुम्हारे साथ टपरी की chai में भी स्वाद ज़्यादा आता है जहां बस तुम दोनो साथ हो,
सुनो क्या करोगी उसके लिए pizza burger बना कर
जबकि उसे तो तुम्हारे हाथ से बनी दाल रोटी में ज़्यादा मिठास आती हैं,
सुनो क्या करोगी खुद को आईने में हर वक्त सवार के,
जबकि प्यार तो उसे तुम्हारी सादगी से ही हैं,
वो परवाह, वो परवानगी से है,
वो इज्ज़त, वो सम्मान से है,
हां प्यार उसे तेरे
व्यवहार से है।

You Are My Dream Come True

Honey... I know my all dreams can't come to true but you are my most beautiful dream come true for rest of my life. My world starts and ends with you my love you are my first thought in the morning and last when I go to bed you are answer to all my prayers. I may not have everything I have ever asked for but you are all I always needed to live this life peacefully. You are my Sukoon.

You are the shadow of my father & brother who loves me the most now for that love I have you.

You are my dream come true with you I want it to share my happiness, my sadness, my emotions and my feelings. Each heartbeat belongs to you baby.

I want to forget my past and enjoy each and every day with you now on. I think we are paired in heaven and your arms are my heaven on heart.

I love you baby.

Prakhar Nema

Prakhar, A person full of positive vibes, comedy is in his blood & writing is his passion.... Helping nature is his strength & social working is one of hobby. Love is not in his life but love is his life in his write-ups... crazy fan of a cute singer & college crush is become his reason of happiness, writing and off course of living such a horrible life in full of chemistry environment.

"वो पन्द्रह मिनिट"

अगस्त का महीना था,
सावन सर-चढ़ कर बोल रहा था
अंधियारी सी छाई थी
पर मैं फिर भी घर से निकला,
कॉलेज जो जाना था
कितना भी कुछ हो गया हो
पर कॉलेज तो लगना ही था
भींगा-भींगा सा मौसम
ऊपर से सर्द हवा
मैंने अपनी छतरी बन्द की
और तुरन्त ही टेक्सी में
आगे बैठ गया
पानी ऊपर से और बाजू से
मुझे भिगोए जा रहा था
फिर मेरी नज़र टेक्सी में
लगे साइड मिरर पर पड़ी
ऐसा लगा जैसे वो बैठी हो
जिसका अक्स में अपने
सपनों में अक्सर देखा करता था,
वो पीछे दाहिनी तरफ बैठी थी
बिल्कुल दरवाजे के किनारे पर
और बारिश की बूंदों के साथ
अपने हाँथों से अठखेलियाँ कर
रही थी,
कभी बूंदे एकदम उसके चहरे पर
आ पड़ती तो कभी उसके दुपट्टे
को छूती हुई निकल जाती
ऐसा लगता जैसे पानी उसके

साथ खेल रहा हो
जैसे ही पानी उसके नाजुक
चेहरे पर पड़ता उसकी आंखें बंद हो जाती
मानो वो अहसास को महसूस कर
रही हो,
यूँ खेलते खेलते वो बाहर ही देखती
वो वादियाँ देख रही थी या वादियाँ उसे
कुछ समझ नहीं आ रहा था
कभी हाथों को बाहर निकाल कर
पानी की बूँदों को संजोती
तो कभी बिखेर देती
ऐसा लगभग पन्द्रह मिनिट
तक चलता रहा
और मैं उस पल को अंदर ही अंदर
समेटता रहा
पन्द्रह मिनिट बाद कॉलेज आ गया
और जैसे ही मैं टेक्सी से उतरा
मैंने किसी और का चेहरा पाया उस लड़की में
अब ये मेरा वहम था या कुछ और
मुझे नहीं पता
पर वो पन्द्रह मिनिट में
ता उम्र नहीं भूल सकता
वो पल मेरे दिल में
हमेशा-हमेशा के लिए घर कर गया.....

Niharika N Jain

Niharika is a writer from tumkur,Karnataka.She also writes in kannada and hindi. Niharika is an engineering student by profession. She believes that words are the best way to Express our inner feelings.

"Rosella"

Eyes are thirst to see you
Hands are eager to hug
Heartbeat increases....
Wait is no longer resisted
Happiness has no limit
Excitement is at peaks...
Flowers start to blossom
Birds start to sing
My Rosella is finally coming....

Lost Love

I don't think love can ever be lost!!!...
because the people whom we love may leave us but that love wont!!
love is a Stubborn creature according to me ...
Life without love is Miserable I agree...
but I don't think life without love even exist ...

Afifa Sharif

Afifa Sharif, born and brought up in Patna, Bihar. Currently she is pursuing BA (Hons) English from Amity University, Lucknow campus. She loves to read and write poetry. She is also interested in different genres of literature from Middle age to post modernism through Gothic, romantics, feminism, fantasy and many more. She is a dynamic in her writings. Apart from this, she is an imaginator in her real life as well, expert in intellectual works. Afifa never fails to motivate others through her word. You can catch her vibes on instagram @irresistible_._phoenix as well as on twitter Afifa Shariff.

Proposed

He proposed me, and I kept my bet,
To be his soulmate and to see our mutual mindset.
Started telling my dreams, those words of unsaid.
I said,
I don't want expensive gifts nor I'm interested how much you're qualified.
I'm least interested about tagging me on social media as well.
But I just want,
Time, I want you to be my side.
I want you to take me a land of dreams where the wounds of my soul can heal.
I just want your warm hugs around me
I want your faith in me whenever I feel low.
I want your affection to encourage me whenever I feel like I'm alone.
I want trust, where you can trust me even if I talk to some strangers with a smile.
I want freedom.
I want care, where you handle me without any lie
I want a beautiful bond where we can tease each other and laugh ridiculously without any fear.
I want you as my best friend, where I can share the burdens of my hurdles.
Can you love me so much so that I can feel like I'm in another world, the world of you and me?
The world of love, care, understanding, trust, loyalty; can I expect these things dear.
You're way too immature to love, these were his words.
I smiled and I got the answer of my quest.
Maybe I'm immature to know world's greatest zest.

I'll fill loyalty, comfort, warmth and fragrance in your wounds,
And will love your scars with all my heart.

Yachika Rathore

Yachika Rathore is a college student who loves poetry. She is fond of writing poems and other stuff.

My Heart Beats For You

Heartbeat which I can feel and feel that I could see you after closing my eyes.
So come close to my eyes and let me see the shine in the dark.
Shine that will free me from the devout soul.
Soul connects me with you and makes me feel happy.
Happiness exists on every inch of my skin when you are with me.
Your existence lets me live in your dreams.
Dreams that truly heals my wounds, 'Given by you '.
' Given by you ' - means why you left me alone in this world.
When nobody was there for me, at that time you were with me.

Now it hurts like a flower.
It makes me feel like you were the petals of roses and this world is thorn.

Come back to me.
Pray from God, let my heartbeat stops from now.
From this moment, let them (our heart) beat "in our world".

Sudipta

A sensitive and passionate soul. Loves being in nature. She hails from Assam.

Love

I long for a safe and peaceful place,
A place that lies in a man's heart;
Safeguarding and healing me
While we build out of love
Beautiful small nests of love,
Painting our inner world with hues of red
Just like blood flowing through our veins;
Where our eyes never cease to meet each other,
Even in the moments of despair
I don't have to struggle for a safe haven
And can rest peacefully in his heart.

Petrichor

It's raining outside.
I'm sitting by my window
And watching the raindrops
Falling on earth with passion.
The eternal petrichor is lingering
And proving their true love.
The raindrops remind me of you
How you made love to me,
Your sweet love essence and sweat
Falling on my body passionately,
We both smelling of love
Yet we couldn't create petrichor.

Collywobbles

Come, sit by my side,
And from the world we hide;
We sit on a bench in the park,
Our eyes enlightened with a spark;
We get closer to each other,
Exchange kisses where nobody can bother,
We forget our worries and troubles
And immerse in a love that gives us collywobbles.

Mohana Priya.S.K

Mohana priya.S.K, a literature student has written many poems, quotes and short story under the pen name called "MONA". All of her works are simple, humorous, understandable and raising questions. She started writing her works at the age of 19.

Attachment In Life.

The beautiful attachment between parents will be true one, though they may be strict or jovial but their love will be true.

Getting attached too much to anyone might make strong your relationship or might hurt your feelings.

If you're feeling hurt and painful then why do you trust people easily am getting attached?
Better be a non- attachment pupil.

Aliya Siddiqua

Aliya Siddiqua. An alluring girl, pursuing her 12th standard bipc. She is from Hyderabad Telangana, she is co-author of 4 books and believe in karma, and love to write, in future She can be an author for sure , and interest in singing.Her curiosity level is high she doesn't know why, because she has my own cup of shy. My insta id is https://www.instagram.com/invites/contact/?i=fwoyvks0x83j&utm_content=hsatuit
My yq I'd: https://www.yourquote.in/aliaa-siddiqua2-bwsbx/quotes/

Felt For You.

Nothing is greedy, no more stricky ,
Will go through any of the lively,
You felted everything which no one can,
You are the one who never get bored,
You know how to react or to do,
The things you only knew,
Stuck on you,
Felt and the feelings that I have,
Would never I have told cz I felt,
My strength and the power,
You know very well I am good and loyal,
My mom you the best and worth,
An I can't keep myself busy, because you are the one who is the best.

No More Words Because It's Just Felt

Can't be describe, the love and affection,
Toward the love ones,
No more words left to describe the truth,
Cause I don't want to lose,
Words are connected, but can't be describe at one's,
The contact throughout the eye is only live,
Feelings takes more,
Time to describe,
The attachment that I felt, the love towards you, but no one else,
Stuck on you,
Parents you the just not the parents of the child,
You the one who, know everything about the child,
Words can't describe the truth of mine,
Cause I know that it's takes time.

Mausam Agrawal

She is 23 year old girl from Nepal.She loves writing poems,stories and shayaris.

बेवजह

उसने पूछा मुझसे
कि तुम्हें मोहब्बत हुई है क्या?
खोए खोए लगते हो
बेवजह ही हंसते हो।

कि उसे समझाएं कौन
ये उसके होने का असर है
ना दिखे तो उसे ढूंडना
हर वक्त उसके ख्यालों में खोना
उसके होने पर सुकून का होना

उसके रूठने पर
सब अधूरा सा लगना
अकेले बैठे-बैठे भी सिर्फ
उसके ख्यालों में खो ना
बेवजह हसना
बेख्याली में भी उसकी बातें करना
सब उससे इश्क का असर है।

Dikshita Singh

Dikshita singh is 2nd year student of BA Hons, she is from Uttar Pradesh, start writing from march 2020, co-author in 5 books, apart from this she is a fashion influencer and she always write her feelings in her writing.

तुम्हारे साथ हर पल

हमसफ़र ना सही कुछ पल का साथ ही दे दिया होता.. ज़िन्दगी भर का नहीं पर कुछ पलों का एहसास दे दिया होता। किसने कहा कि दुआएं कबूल होती हैं .. दुआओं में ही तो मांगा था मैंने तुम्हारे साथ ज़िन्दगी भर का सफर .. पर कुछ कदम भी साथ चलना नसीब ना हुआ। मैं ये नहीं कहती कि बेवफा तुम हो बेवफा मेरी किस्मत है जो पास तो आती है फिर ऐसे वक्त में मुंह मोड़ जाती है जब उसे पता होता है कि उसके मुंह मोड़ने पे मेरा दिल टूटेगा.. शायद बेवफाई शब्द मेरी किस्मत के पन्ने पे उस स्याही से लिख गई है जो कभी मिट ना सकेगा.. हां कभी कभार जज्बातों की चादर से थोड़ा धुंधला हो जाता है पर वफादारी तो देखो उसकी खुद को कभी मेरी ज़िन्दगी से ओझल नहीं होने देता.. इसलिए मैंने आज अपनी किस्मत से भी एक बात कह दिया ' यार अगर तुझे जाना है तो जा, रुकना है तो रुक जा.. पर यूं कुछ पल के लिए ओझल होकर मुझे खुश ना किया कर.. क्योंकि बार बार मैं टूट जाऊं और फिर खुद को जोडूं इतनी ताकत और हिम्मत नहीं है मुझमें ' ।

कहा तो मैंने अपनी मोहब्बत से भी कुछ है की ' सुनो.. अब तुम सिर्फ मेरे ख्वाबों में ही साथ रहना.. क्योंकि असल में तुम्हारा साथ शायद मेरे नसीब में नहीं .. पर एक बात कहूं ये दुआ जरूर करूंगी कि तुम लौट आओ..' ' यूं अकेले इन रास्तों पर छोड़ रहे हो और बिना वजह अपना रुख मोड़ रहे हो.. '

काश यह एहसास हो तुम्हे की कितनी मोहब्बत है मुझे तुमसे.. पर हां अगर फिर भी ना आए तो कोई बात नहीं कुछ महीनों की यादों में पूरी ज़िन्दगी गुज़ार लूंगी क्योंकि तुम्हारे सिवा किसी और को आंख उठा कर के भी नहीं देखूंगी.. तुम्हे तो यह पता ही है वादे तोड़ना मुझे आता नहीं ।

चलो चलती हूं अगर कभी याद आए तो बिना सोचे याद कर लेना क्योंकि मेरे लिए मेरी ज़िन्दगी का हिस्सा तुम हमेशा रहोगे।

Ajay Gupta

Ajay Gupta is from Ambekdkar Nagar District Uttar Pradesh. He is currently pursuing B.tech from Dr.Aith Kanpur in Computer Science And Engineering Branch His childhood wish was to do something creative and stand out of the crowd. Currently he is working on web development projects. He has a keen interest in capturing nature(photography) and writing as well.
Instagram handles: @thug_ajay @cool_photography_drawing @kaviyon_ki_awaz

।।।यादेँ।।।

तेरे जाने के बाद,मै और मेरी तन्हाई अक्सर एक दूसरे से बातें करते रहते हैं।
कि अगर तुम होती तो ऐसा होता,तुम होती तो वैसा होता।
हम तुमसे कुछ कहते ,तुम हमसे कुछ कहती।
मुझे तेरा दीदार होता, तुझे मेरा दीदार होता।
ये रातें तुम्हारे खुली जुल्फों की यादेँ हैं,
तुम्हारी आंचल की चमक के आगे ,सितारो के चमक भी सादे हैं।
ये हवा का झोंका तुम्हारे होने का अहसास कराती है,
इन पत्तियों की सरसराहट तुम्हारी बातों की याद दिलाती है।
सोचता हूँ मैं कब से गुमसुम,तुम नही हो,
मगर मेरा दिल कहता है,तुम यही हो।
काश!! तुम यहाँ होती,
तो कुछ ऐसा होता,कुछ वैसा होता,
हम तुमसे कुछ कहते ,तुम हमसे कुछ कहती।

Mohanapriya.K

Co-author Mohanapriya.K is a budding writer from Tamilnadu, India. She has completed her Bachelor's degree in Engineering stream. She has been a writer for one year as her passion. She wants to be a best compiler and voice over artist in future. She has been co-author of 75+ anthologies so far. She participated in many writing contests on instagram and received certificates. Yet she sincerely hope that this writing journey of her will continue as sweetly as it is now and will bring her many successes. You can find her writings on her instagram page.

Instagram : @colours_honey_official
E-mail : doraa.kutty@gmail.com

Attachment With My Pet

Our love for our pets is so much more than we see heaven in this world.
Because they have many times more affection for us than we show for them
Will give.
There can be no other music in this world sweeter than their voice.
Nor can there be anything else in this world that can compensate for their love.
Anything else that parallels their love will definitely never be compensated.
I have faith in miracles.
When a miracle happens in life unexpectedly.
The pets are similar.
It is very important that we first understand ourselves as we are.
And although we do not understand, we must do our best to make sure that whoever we show our face to is in the way others treat us.
And that we love ourselves as much as we love others.
Pets will definitely help us with this.
The smile on my face would bloom as soon as I saw him.
The same goes for him.
I love my pet so much.
Love your pets too.
Live your life very happily with your pets.
Only then will they incorporate you into their world.
And will join and want to join in our life.
I loved alot my puppy.
Because there is nothing in this world that is higher than the blessing, he shows me.
His slang is one of my favourites.

The relationship between him and me is very sacred.
He and I will feel this very well.
I understand his language very well.
It would seem to me What I would do if they were not with me.
I will feel like I am in heaven when I am with him.
I just named him.
I have no words to describe his beauty!
I miss him so much when he's not around anymore.
My wish is that he should always be with me.
I really appreciate all the work he does.
All the actions he does are my favourites.
He will always be remembered!

Shriyansh Jain

Shriyansh is an architect student and a professional graphic/caricature artist. He draws and know things.

For Once, Please?

Hey beautiful what ya upto
Why am i everyday stalking you
I hope you haven't forgotten me
Can we meet for once please?
'm hush coz i know you can't
But what about our last dance
Your life is on track
You've got friends of yours
But was i an important part?
Ans this - are we done?
If not
Then why does it hurt all upon
We are over
If yes
Then whom you call yours
Here I am ...still waiting
Come soon You are killing!

Adarsh Pandey

This is Adarsh Pandey belongs to Prayagraj, Uttar Pradesh, lives in Mumbai Maharastra. Adarsh is a author specializing in science – fiction and fantasy.. His website is www.writeradarshpandey.com

His published books are:

1. अच्छे निर्णय कै से लें(part1)
2. अच्छा निर्णय कै से लें(part2)

He contributed in the book The Radius as a co-author.

Fear Of Getting Love

I learned that when it comes to sexual relationships, most girls do not understand what is happening. That is because their perspective on this subject is completely different from that of boys. Often a girl says to justify sex, "but I love her." Even if she doesn't want to get into that relationship with him. Why does this happen? Girls resort to sex to get love and boys resort to love to get sex.It works like this: the girl dreams of ever marrying a boy. The boy dreams of everything he wants to do with the girl before going back to his friends. The girl's conscience tells her that it is right to do soWhile the boy's conscience tells him to the contrary, he moves on. Why? Of course for physical pleasure. But I think there is another reason for this: it makes him feel like a man. But there is a big irony in it, where did masculinity come from in deceiving a woman? Something I have discovered and that is that when you honour a woman, you honor yourself. Why? Because someday you will regret it and regret always lasts longer than pleasure. In Rob Roy's movie, the actor who plays the lead says Reputation is a gift a man gives to himself. When you give prestige (which is best for her) to a woman knowing that what you are doing is right according to your heart, you honor yourself. You make it safe that you will never have to live life with regrets.The girl dreams of ever getting married to a boy. The boy dreams of everything he wants to do with the girl before going back to his friends.The girl's conscience tells him that it is the right thing to do, while the boy's conscience tells him to the contrary, yet he moves on. Why? Of course for physical pleasure. But I think there is another reason for this: it makes him feel like a man. But there is a big irony in it, where did masculinity come from in deceiving a woman?

मेरा प्यार

मैंने सोचा भी ना था ।
की इक्स मुझे भी होगा।
मौला इक्स हुआ भी तो कैसा हुआ।।
की वो मेरे दिल के अंदर है पर जमी पे नही।
सपने हम मिलकर देखे थे ।
साथ निभायेंगे सात जन्मों का ।।
वो आसमा पे और हम जमी पर रह गए ।।

Amit Pandit

Amit Pandit belongs to Bhopal (MP). He is an Electronics & instrumentation engineer and works as a Power plant Automation Engineer at Sagar Group. His hobbies include writing Poetry, Poetry and Poetry. He is a published poet."He contributed in the books titled The Radius, Melting Hearts and many as a co-author"

अहसास पन्नों में लिख लिए कविता बन गई,
और लिर प्रेम भी तन एक अनहि कल्पना ही है.!

वो राधा हम श्याम

दोनो ही संग बदनाम हुए
वो राधा ओर हम श्याम हुए
मुरली वाले के नाम थी वो
और हम उसके नाम हुए

प्रेम कहां आसान हुआ
बस बंधन आठोंयाम हुए
पूर्ण हुई जब धनुष प्रतिज्ञा
तब मिथिला के राम हुए.

एक तरफ़!

सूरज की पांख़ें एक तरफ़
पीपल की सांखें एक तरफ़,
ये सारी दुनिया एक तरफ़
और उसकी आंखें एक तरफ़!

Poonam Choudhary

Poonam Choudhary, an Orator by profession, Language and Soft Skill trainer for the last 14 years & Digital Marketer, adopted writing as a hobby. Her passion for languages and keen observation made her start her career as a writer. She strongly believes that writing is the most dominated way of expressing one's ideas, thoughts and beliefs.

Stuck Or.........Hallucination??

Life is a vicious circle of Happiness and Sadness and perfect notion that fits here is “The show must go on”. So, does life Ever allow us to stuck on anything??? Or, is it actually giving us time for the lessons which are yet to be learnt out of a specific situation?

Well, what’s your say on that??

Hmmmm…. I think, if life is letting you stuck on something for a while or a specific duration of time which is beyond your control, where you feel like, you can neither get out of it nor tolerate it, which actually makes you feel STUCK…...and at times forces you to get overexcited or panic or angry or impatient and let you experience hell lot of mood swings…. then it means that the desired lessons learnt out of that situation are not enough. There is something more to it which God wants you to explore and the destiny would unveil the same, in due course of time.

So, Now the question that arises here is, how should we react in such situations?? How can we take control of our emotions??? Shall we go with the wind or fight against it???? Shall we get impulsive or sit back and wait for the right time when things will fall at its right place on its own, with no reaction to it, which might take little longer as well than usual time.

I am sure……you must be encountering such questions only, Isn’t it??

Albert Einstein has said, “The significant problems we have cannot be solved at the same level of thinking with which we have created them.”

So, in order to overcome any impediment of life we have to change our perspective towards the same. We have to find out, what that specific situation is really demanding from us. Somewhere, our inner conscious knows it but we don’t accept

it due to some kind of fear. But trust me when you challenge your fears and find that good thing in that particular situation, which can let you soar the sky, the game will change. Then you will start enjoying it and realize which thing you have to invest your energy in. Is it Love or Hatred? Failures or success? Problems or Solutions? Blame Game or Team-building?? You will see yourself, overlooking the crap and focusing only on the manifestation of the real Success & happiness of life.

It's never the situation that's at fault. It's the way you choose to look at it.

Simmy

chirping girl , simmy belongs from Ludhiana,punjab .she loves to pen emotions and reality.she writes to express herself. Her Instagram handle is @loovvee_feelings.

मेरा इश्क तू

मेरा इश्क तू,
मेरी जान तू,
मेरे भीतर का प्यार तू,
मेरे अंदर का तूफान तू,
मेरे हर लफ्ज़ की पहचान तू,
मेरे हर शब्द की जान तू,
मेरी चाह भी तू,
मेरा राज़ भी तू,
मेरे दिल की पहचान तू,
मेरी खुशी की वजह है तू,
मेरी हसी, मेरी मुस्कान तू
मेरा इश्क तू,
मेरी जान तू,
मेरी हर धड़कन का शाज़ है तू,
मेरी चाहत का पैग़ाम है तू,
मेरी सांसों की सरगम है तू,
मेरे खयालों का दर्पण है तू,
क्या कहूं! क्या करूं!
दिल की ही मैं सुनूं
मेरा इश्क मेरी जान तू जान तू
मेरा सबसे बड़ा राज़ तू।।

Divas Vishwajna. C

Divas Vishwajna. C who is a student of Aeronautical engineering Diploma. He lives in Bangalore but basically he is from Chikmaglure . He loves traveling and writing is his biggest strength.

Journey

A reddy and rao 2 large family were looking for a reservation in a platform number 5 at Bangalore kempegowda railway station. The rao family members were calling Krishna. And Divya from reddy's family collected her ticket and her family said, don't worry we will be coming soon...as you know your granny need's us my lovely girl right...? She took that ticket from her aunt and went to fill water. Krishana was in hurry and he collided with Divya and the he apologized her .she said its fine and he went near his family Krishna's mom Kala gave him a ticket, as he saw the ticket

Krishan:- hey..mummeeeee, this is not faaair...!

Kala :- you would have come earlier and grab your seat's

Krishna's aunty :- hey you get lost... Loffer..!

Krishna:- a great time comes I'll take revange on you guys

Krishna's aunt :- go now (with a smile)

Krishna was in search for his seat all of a sudden he again collided with the same girl.

Divya:- hey..

are you playing or what.? And you have been following me since from then.

Krishan:- vooo cool down actually 'Iam sorry' and I'm not following you I am in search of my seat now and at that time I was in hurry so sorry again..!

Divya :- what ever...!

Krishna got the top most sleeper seat and that was opposite to Divya's seat aloted. krishna waved his hand. She replied with a smile and that's how their friendship started as the journey was 3 days long to kashi their attachment started growing and number exchanged some how. Iam Divu going kanyakumari to their marriage . .!

Ankitha:- even iam traveling to kanyakumari.. wait they both met exactly the same way as we both met.. ! Wow what a coincidence..

And then I continued the story to her

Hetavi Singh

Hetavi Singh is a Student and pursuing her graduation From Mumbai University.The coauthor loves to read books.Author hobbies are mainly studies.Drawing ,Sketching,photography and editing are some of the fields of interest of the author.Uncertainty by "Hetavi Singh" is a modest attempt by the poet to juxtapose the complexity and human life vis-Ã -vis the simplicity .The author is working on building her career goals .you can read her published book such as "Appealing","Scarlet wings","Vivid". Find her on
instagram @mixed_handedness
And.. website:learngrowyourway.blogspot.com

"Attachment"

Did you see,the love in your girl eyes it's attachment!!.
the source of all suffering,
young to aged it's attachment!! .
disappointment and pain when you fail it's attachment!!.
Because we imagined different,some recover fast or late,it's attachment!!.
attachment to things that we mistakenly see as permanent,it's attachment!!.
That what leads to jealousy when your friend with your guy it's attachment!!.
The shadow of greed that's
attachment!!.
temporary
emotions, thoughts, people, and scenery.
just flow with it,Its attachments!!
To let go of everything
lose , it's attachment!!.
You only lose what you cling to just leave it,cause it is attachment!!.
dependency , is attachment!!.
views impediment to the spiritual path,is attachment!!.
purest love and it is within,its attachments !!.

Prachi Sharma

She is Prachi Sharma. She lived in Ghaziabad district in U. P. She pursing Bsc maths from CCS UNIVERSITY. She participated in more than 30 anthologies. She wrote a book FEELING IN WORDS available on Google Play store. She compiled three anthologies WRITE TO FEEL NOT TO EXPLAIN, WRITER'S WORLD and FIRST DAY. She participated in Record anthologies and as a co-author. She is the founder of KAVYANJALI. This is an online platform who provide opportunities for writers and develop their skills.

Give your feedback on
email (prachisharma51689@gmail.com).
Instagram id (@sharma0162).

Connection

Yes, still any connection is left.
Yes, some connection we have
Don't know what
But we still meet up
When we don't want to saw your face.
Again and again we meet
I saw you without any reason
After a break
We meet without any reason
Yes, something is left between us
God wants to complete
What, we have to find?

Manya Bansal

Manya is an explorer of art, music, philosophy and dreams. She wants to paint all her dreams into poetry or painting. She currently has her art page @artistique_secrets where you can see her heart. She is a silent writer who keeps her writings very private.

Unromantic

It was all Unromantic Our love wasn't, isn't and will not going to be sweet or romantic. It is not the one with cute or funny nicknames and definitely not the one with some kind of song which we call "OURS". There is no promise and no string attached, we don't even know if we will going to get married, if we will going to share same name plate or if we will going to have identical keys. You are not the last piece of my puzzle and I am not the light at the end of your tunnel. Yes, we are in love but probably it will change its course of time in the middle and who knows that we will be living in different cities, dying in different time zones. We won't be looking at the shooting stars sitting on the roof, we won't be the eternal lovers like Radha Krishna. I guess we don't need each other to keep our love alive. We will grow with time. But when we take last breath I want it should be written like a mythology because even Radha did not ended up with Krishna still we worship their love like it is a religion

Flairs and Glairs, a platform by a student for the students. We are esteemed youth struggling to carve out our path for our future and we follow a basic mindset Since everyone is not born with all-round skills. Joining hands with people who are born to execute it with perfection is the best way to evolve. Self-Evolution is the need of the hour but, evolving as a community is what we strive for. The initiative as kickstarted by, Founder- Mr. Shubham Shah with the motive to utilize the skillset and talent of writing has now a team of 10+ people who are actively participating into newer forms of learning and discovering talents among youngsters. We Provide platform and services like Publishing opportunities, Open mics, Workshops, Hands-on training. Operating with Brand Name of Flairs and Glairs (Publication House), we offer the chance of elevating a passionate writer to an esteemed author With Brand name Teekhe Zasbaaat. We bring to you an opportunity to get accustomed with the Public Speaking and Presenting of Thoughts along with regular challenges to brush up your inking spirit. The newest initiative to extend our services we introduced in a new writing Platform- The Glittering Fables and Ink Over Tears.

We Choose to Fly Like A Falcon than to be

a Leg Pulling Crab.

To Know More: Infoline – 7781900870
Mail Us At-
flairsandglairs@gmail.com / info@flairsandglairs.in
Or Visit is at
www.flairsandglairs.com / www.flairsandglairs.in
Social Handles- @flairsandglairs @teekhezasbaaat

www.ingramcontent.com/pod-product-compliance
Ingram Content Group UK Ltd.
Pitfield, Milton Keynes, MK11 3LW, UK
UKHW022004190726
13853UKWH00004B/1735